For Jimmy James and Rosie ~ SL

For Tom and Sam ~ BC

LITTLE TIGER PRESS LTD,
An imprint of the Little Tiger Group
1 Coda Studios, 189 Munster Road,
London SW6 6AW
www.littletiger.co.uk

First published in Great Britain 2003
as **3, 2, 1 Bedtime**
This edition published 2019

A CIP catalogue record for this book is available from the British Library

 • 978-1-78881-519-2

Printed in China

LTP/2700/2736/0319

10 9 8 7 6 5 4 3 2 1

This stinky book belongs to:

SUPER SPUD AND THE Stinky Space Rescue!

Sam Lloyd Ben Cort

LITTLE TIGER
LONDON

In a galaxy far, far away,
Spud's alien friends were
getting ready for bed.

"Rip roaring rockets!" Spud
gasped. "What a mess!
They need my help!"

This was a mission for . . .

SUPERHERO SPACEBOY

SPUD!

POW! SLAM! Spud landed on planet Whiff.

"Rip roaring rockets!" he gasped. "What a stink!"

"Pong, pong, pong," nodded the aliens. "We need a bath. Will you help us?"

So Spud washed and scrubbed and scrubbed and washed until the aliens were all clean and ready for bed.

"Nighty, nighty, sleepy tighty,"
whispered Spud. But his mission
was not complete.
Spud fired up
his rocket.
3, 2, 1, BLAST OFF!
SUPERHERO SPACEBOY SPUD
TO THE RESCUE!

POW! SLAM! Spud landed on planet Fuzz.

"Rip roaring rockets!" he gasped. "What a tangle!"

"Frizz, frizz, frizz," squeaked the alien. "Will you help me brush my hair?"

So Spud brushed and combed and combed and brushed until the alien's hair was neat and tidy, ready for bed.

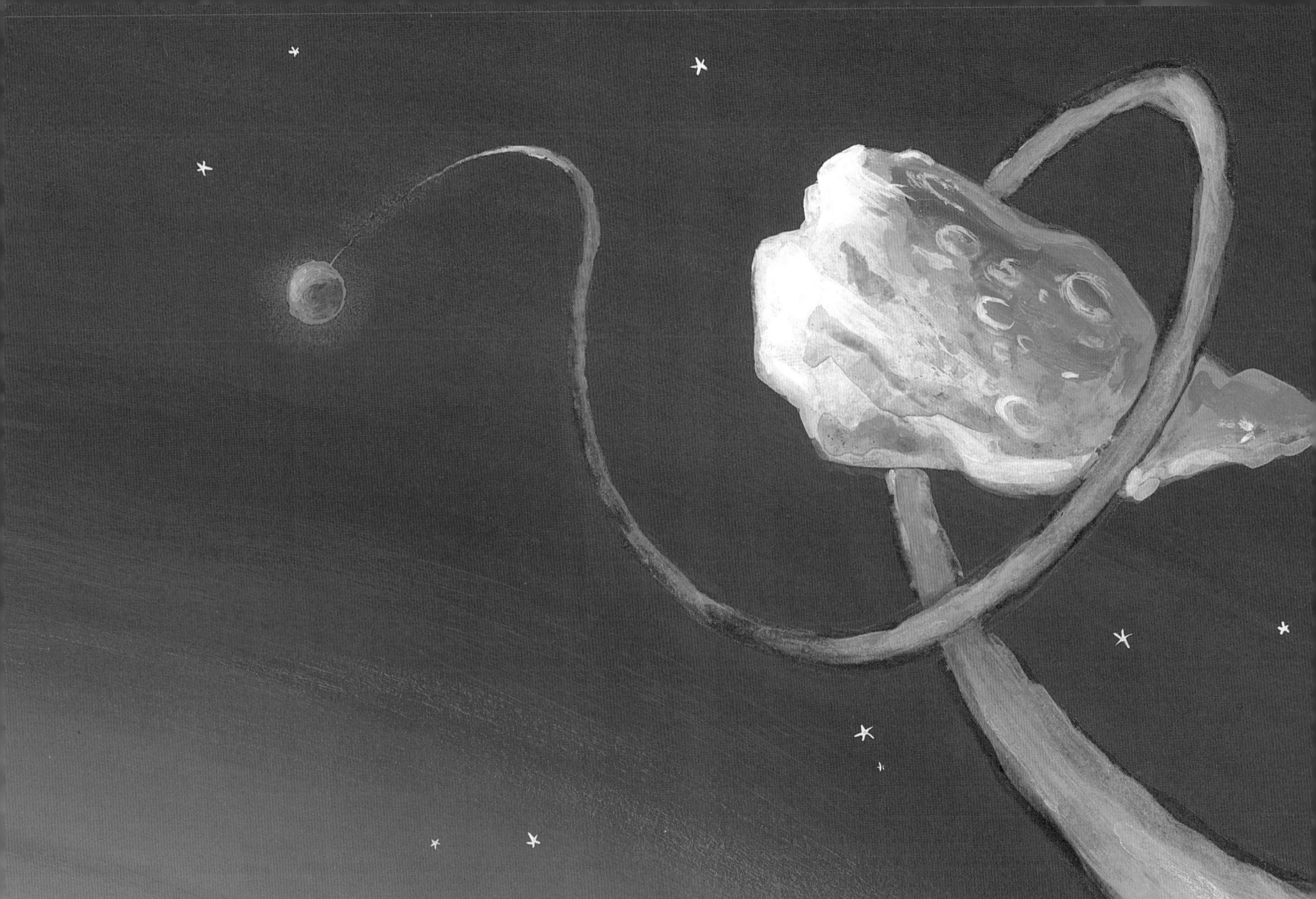

“Nighty, nighty, sleepy tighty,” whispered Spud. But his mission was not complete. Spud fired up his rocket.

3, 2, 1, BLAST OFF!

SUPERHERO SPACEBOY SPUD TO THE RESCUE!

POW! SLAM! Spud landed on planet Piddle.

"Rip roaring rockets!" he gasped. "What an awful accident!"

"Pee, pee, pee," nodded the aliens. "We need to do a wee. Help us, Super Spud!"

So Spud helped the little
aliens to go to the toilet.

"Nighty, nighty, sleepy tighty," whispered Spud. But still his mission was not complete. Spud fired up his rocket.
3, 2, 1, BLAST OFF!
SUPERHERO SPACEBOY SPUD TO THE RESCUE!

POW! SLAM! Spud landed on planet Fang.

"Rip roaring rockets!" he gasped. "Those teeth are filthy! You need to clean them."

"Gnash, gnash, gnash," nodded the alien with a smile.

So Spud brushed and polished
and polished and brushed until
the alien's teeth were shiny
and sparkling, ready for bed.

At last the mission was complete. All the aliens were tucked up in bed.

"Nighty,

nighty,

sleepy . . .

tighty . . ."

yawned Spud and climbed on his rocket.

Superhero Spaceboy Spud to HOME!

Spud curled up snug in his own bed.
"Well done," smiled his mummy.
"It's a tough job being a superhero."
She leaned forward and gave
him a kiss. "Nighty, nighty, sleepy
tighty," she whispered . . .

But Superhero Spaceboy Spud
was already fast asleep.

The end

More stinky books

from Little Tiger Press!

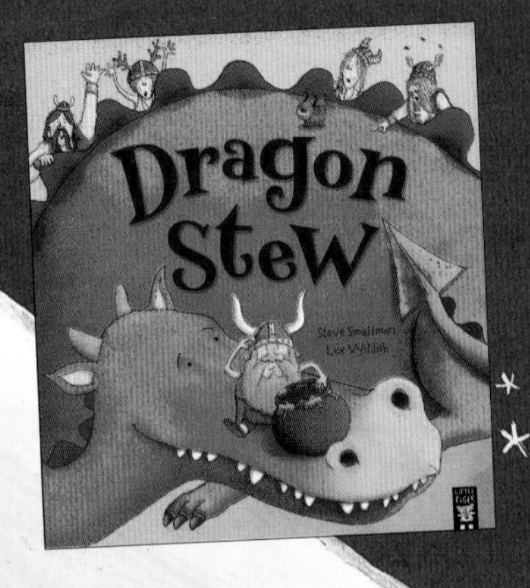

For information regarding any of the above titles or
for our catalogue, please contact us: Little Tiger Press Ltd,
1 Coda Studios, 189 Munster Road, London SW6 6AW
Tel: 020 7385 6333, Fax: 020 7385 7333, E-mail: contact@littletiger.co.uk
www.littletiger.co.uk